POLLINATOR PALS

HAZEL THE HONEYBEE POLLINATES

by Rebecca Donnelly
illustrated by Dean Gray

GRASSHOPPER

Tools for Parents & Teachers

Grasshopper Books enhance imagination and introduce the earliest readers to fiction with fun storylines and illustrations. The easy-to-read text supports early reading experiences with repetitive sentence patterns and sight words.

Before Reading

- Discuss the cover illustration. What do they see?
- Look at the glossary together. Discuss the words.

Read the Book

- Read the book to the child, or have him or her read independently.
- "Walk" through the book and look at the illustrations. Who is the main character? What is happening in the story?

After Reading

- Prompt the child to think more. Ask: What is Hazel's job in the hive? If you were a honeybee, which job would you want to have? Why?

Grasshopper Books are published by Jump!
5357 Penn Avenue South
Minneapolis, MN 55419
www.jumplibrary.com

Library of Congress Cataloging-in-Publication Data

Names: Donnelly, Rebecca, author.
Gray, Dean, illustrator.
Title: Hazel the honeybee pollinates / by Rebecca Donnelly;
illustrated by Dean Gray.
Description: Minneapolis, MN: Jump!, Inc., [2022]
Series: Pollinator pals
Includes reading tips and supplementary back matter.
Audience: Ages 7-10.
Identifiers: LCCN 2021000103 (print)
LCCN 2021000104 (ebook)
ISBN 9781636902319 (hardcover)
ISBN 9781636902326 (paperback)
ISBN 9781636902333 (ebook)
Subjects: LCSH: Readers (Primary)
Honeybee–Juvenile fiction.
Classification: LCC PE1119.2 .D674 2022 (print)
LCC PE1119.2 (ebook)
DDC 428.6/2–dc23
LC record available at https://lccn.loc.gov/2021000103
LC ebook record available at https://lccn.loc.gov/2021000104

Editor: Eliza Leahy
Direction and Layout: Anna Peterson
Illustrator: Dean Gray

Printed in the United States of America at
Corporate Graphics in North Mankato, Minnesota.

Table of Contents

Bees and Blossoms

Hi, I'm Hazel! I'm a honeybee.

I live in a hive with thousands of other bees. I'm a forager. I find nectar and pollen to feed everyone in my hive.

In the hive, bees do a waggle dance to show others where to find the best flowers. The dance tells me which way to go and how far to fly. Today, I'm going to the apple orchard. Come with me!

I love to fly! I have two sets of wings. They move so fast they make a buzzing sound. *Buzz!* I fly over farms, fields, and gardens.

wing

Here is the orchard! The apple trees have many blossoms. I will land on the blossom that smells the best.

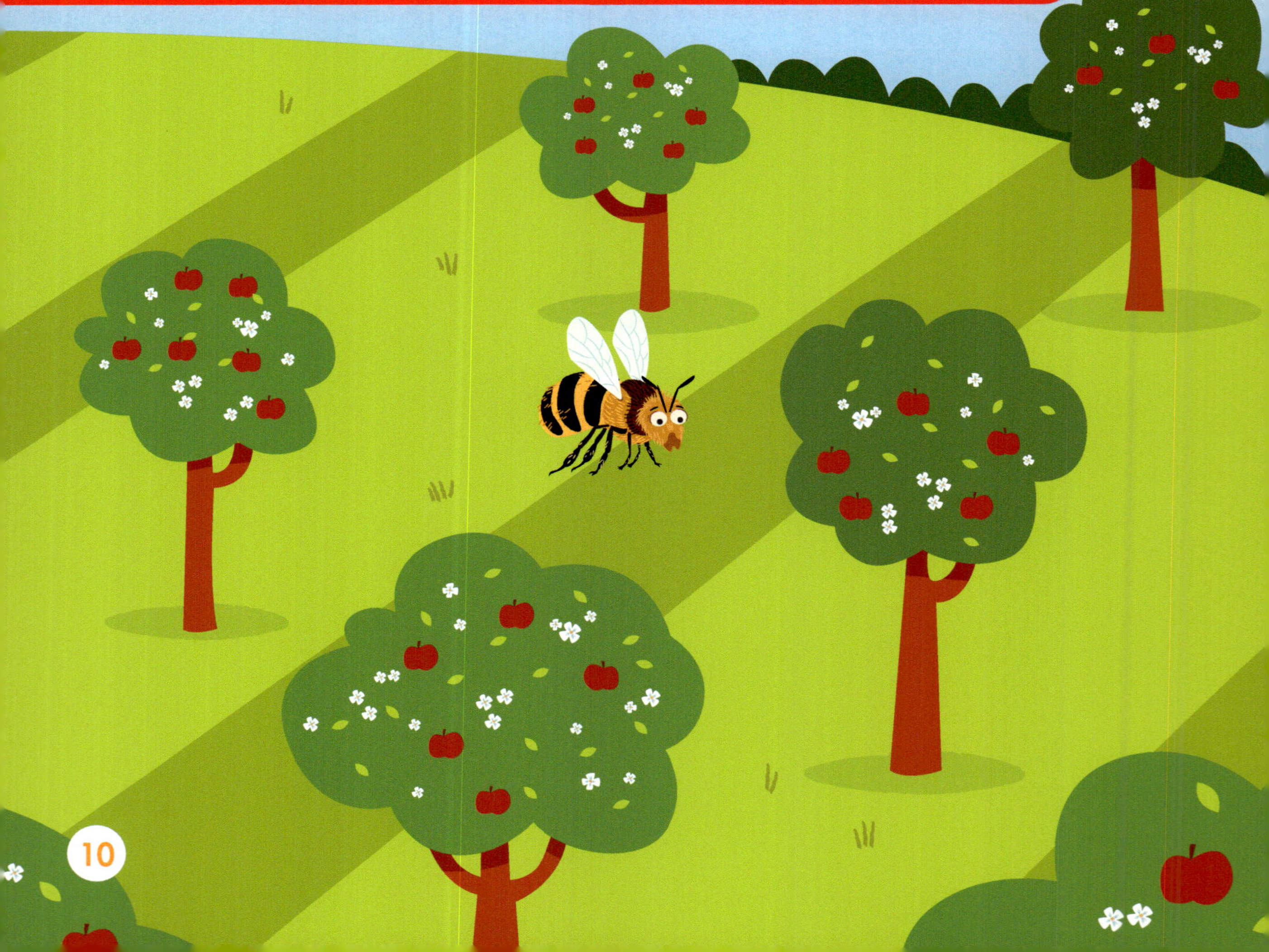

I drink nectar with my long tongue. Tiny hairs on my tongue trap it. Then I swallow it. Yum! I choose another blossom. I carry the nectar in my crop.

Pollen sticks to me each time I land on a blossom. I use my front legs to brush it onto my back legs. That is how I carry it home. I can make twelve trips each day. I can carry four times my weight in pollen in one day!

pollen

Buzz! Off to another flower! Some of the pollen rubs off. This is how I pollinate plants. Soon, apples will grow.

I look for other kinds of flowers. These dandelions look yummy!

Hey, it's Molly the mason bee! Molly doesn't live in a hive like I do. She lives alone in a log. Molly gathers nectar, too.

log

I bring nectar to my hive. We use it to make honey! All bees drink nectar and spread pollen, but only honeybees make honey.

Worker bees store nectar and pollen in cells. Architect bees make wax to cover the cells.

architect bee
worker bee
wax

Soon, the nectar turns into honey. We eat it during the long winter. Nurse bees feed pollen to our young.

On my next trip, I'll look for more nectar and pollen. I can pollinate 5,000 blossoms a day! That makes me a very busy bee.

Let's Review!

How do bees pollinate apple trees? Let's take a look at Hazel's journey!

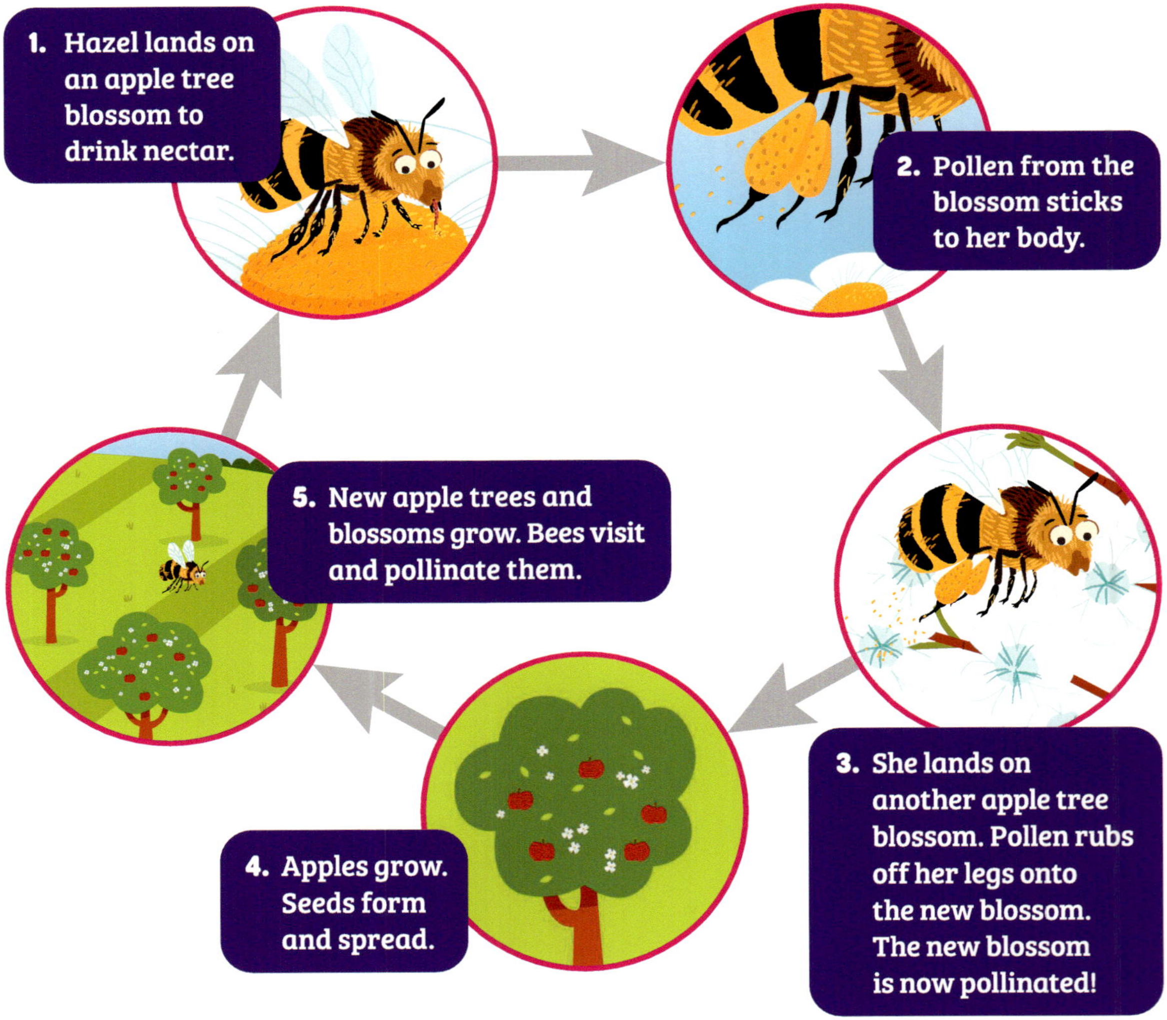

Where European Honeybees Live

Hazel is a European honeybee. These bees are found around the world. Take a look!

■ = where European honeybees live

To Learn More

Finding more information is as easy as 1, 2, 3.

1. Go to www.factsurfer.com
2. Enter "**Hazelthehoneybeepollinates**" into the search box.
3. Choose your book to see a list of websites.

Glossary

blossoms: Flowers on trees and bushes.

cells: The six-sided structures made of wax where honeybees lay eggs and store food.

crop: A special organ in a bee's abdomen that is used to carry nectar.

forager: A worker bee that leaves the hive to gather nectar and pollen.

hive: A structure in which bees live and raise their young.

nectar: A sweet liquid made by flowers to attract pollinators.

orchard: A group of fruit or nut trees planted for harvesting.

pollen: A powder made by the male parts of plants.

pollinate: To take pollen from the male part of a flower and put it on the female part of a flower so the plant can reproduce.

wax: A thick substance made by bees to build cells in a hive.

Index